12/09

Augie

Among the lucky ....

You are the chosen ...

for you are as pretty as

my "Favourite"

Always keep the faith!

Always

A. Lion

THE
Adventures
of Shamus O'Malley

The Prophecy of Light

THE
Adventures
of Shamus O'Malley

The Prophecy of Light

written by

JIM KIRKER

illustrated by

SANDRA TRYON

Plymouth Proclamation Press • Plymouth, Michigan
800/783-2026

Plymouth Proclamation Press, Inc.
44644 Ann Arbor Rd., Suite F
Plymouth, Michigan 48170-3908
800/783-2026
Fax: 734/451-2105

Manufactured in Mexico

Library of Congress Cataloging-in-Publication Data

ISBN 1-879709-01-5

For Patrick and Kara

Whose love and friendship, each in their own way, provided the magic to inspire this story.

And for Jack, Kathy, Sandy, "JoJo", and Ana who kept the "faith".

THE ADVENTURES
of Shamus O'Malley
The Prophecy of Light

TABLE OF CONTENTS

A BEGINNING

It Couldn't Happen!

The early dawn in Ireland was fresh with the scent of a thousand flowers. As the sun rose slowly in the blue sky, its warmth and light brought new life and bright colors to all that it bathed. All but the King were still asleep in the Kingdom of the Leprechauns.

King O'Flaherty, up early, decided not to wake anyone else and left the underground Kingdom alone to work in the flower garden that surrounded the Rainbow Tree. He always took great joy in doing all that he could to make each flower grow as beautiful as it could be. As the King began cutting daisies and large buttercups, he reached up to straighten the gold and emerald crown that he wore at all times to protect himself and the Kingdom.

In the quiet and peace of the flower garden, King O'Flaherty did not notice that high in the sky one dark cloud had suddenly appeared, driven by a wind making strange low howling noises. The dark cloud moved ever so quickly in the direction of the King.

1

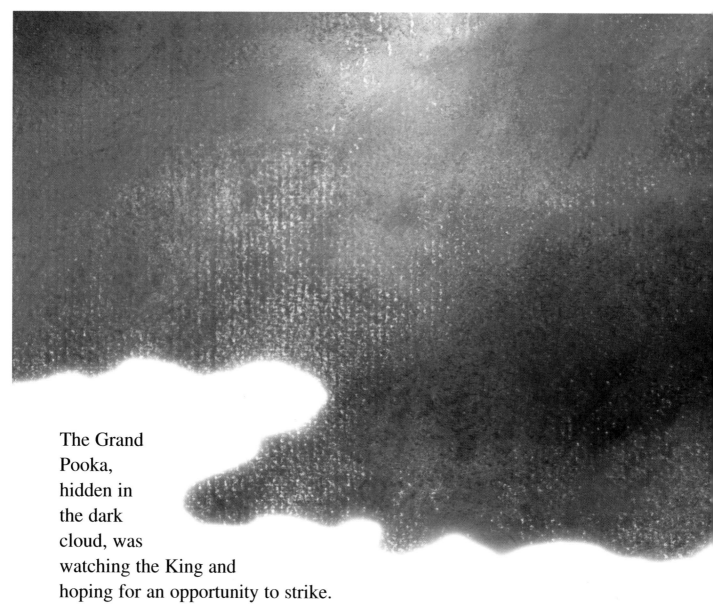

The Grand
Pooka,
hidden in
the dark
cloud, was
watching the King and
hoping for an opportunity to strike.

The Grand Pooka was afraid to strike a leprechaun king wearing the gold and emerald crown. Many years ago the Grand Pooka, the dreaded enemy of the leprechauns, learned of the thousand-year-old legend, called the "Prophecy of Light", handed down secretly over the years by leprechaun kings. According to the legend, the special powers of the leprechaun king's gold and emerald crown came from "One" even more powerful than the Grand Pooka itself. The Grand Pooka desperately wanted this crown.

The King, while
bending over to cut a daisy,
slowly moved his crown back on his head. Just
as he stood up with the daisy, his crown tumbled off his head to the
ground. In an instant the Grand Pooka leaped out of the dark cloud as
a monstrous beast, swooped down, and captured King O'Flaherty and
his crown.

The King, flying high in the grasp of this beast toward an
unknown world, couldn't believe that he had been captured! It
couldn't happen!! King O'Flaherty now knew that the time of the
great battle foretold by the "Prophecy of Light" was near. The words
of the ancient legend were suddenly very real. Sadly, neither he nor
his crown would be there to help the leprechauns.

King O'Flaherty's heart filled with fear and despair, not for
himself, but for all those left behind in his Kingdom...and most of all
for Shamus O'Malley.

3

CHAPTER ONE
PaPa and Christy

Far across the ocean on the Connecticut shoreline, the spring afternoon sun was brilliant, everywhere its rays sparkled off the earth, warming all that they touched. The sky was a soft blue with many small puffy white clouds darting across it. The icy blue Atlantic Ocean stretched out as far as one's eyes could see. Tall beach grass and fields of colorful wild flowers danced to each change in direction of the warm spring breeze.

For Jack O'Shaughnessey this day, like all other days in his life, was special. Jack was a tall, handsome sixty-four year old Irishman with big blue eyes matched only by his large warm smile. He succeeded in life because he had faith in himself and, most importantly, faith in the "God of All". But Jack was not aware that very soon his faith would be tested, perhaps more than even he could bear.

Jack and his wife Sandy had raised a fine family. They had a son John, a daughter Betty, and were blessed with five grand-children:

Amanda, Tim, Michael, Mary and Christy. Jack had retired several years earlier after his wife Sandy had passed away. Being with his grandchildren was now the most important part of Jack's life.

Everyone in the community knew Jack as their fireman, and also as their real-life hero. Many times he had risked his life to save others. Jack's actions showed that he truly understood the meaning of the words, "in giving one receives". The "God of All" had blessed Jack with a unique spirit and gentleness. He had a hearty laugh and a rare talent to tell fascinating stories.

To his grandchildren, Jack O'Shaughnessey was the world's greatest and most loved grandfather. They all adored him, and affectionately called him "PaPa". PaPa was especially close to his youngest granddaughter, Christy O'Shaughnessey... for PaPa was Christy's hero. Even falling snowflakes that touched each other in a snowstorm were not as close to each other as Christy was to her PaPa.

Further down the beach, the same warm breeze blew gently from the ocean through the windows of St. Francis Children's Hospital. The breeze rustled the sheets that partially covered Christy as she sat on her bed. Christy was nine and a half years old, and everyone who saw her agreed that she was cuter than an angel. She had curly blonde hair, green eyes, and cheeks lightly dusted with freckles. Her personality and courage reminded everyone that she was just like her grandfather.

Christy had become very sick. Her doctors had told Christy's Mom and Dad that to have any chance to cure Christy, they would have to treat her, starting today, with a powerful new medicine. Christy was also told by her doctors that at times the medicine would make her body feel terrible all over. Her Mom also warned her that she might even lose some of her pretty blonde hair and that she would find it difficult to eat her favorite foods.

Christy's cheerful spirit was not affected by her sickness. This was because PaPa had taught her that as long as she kept her courage and faith in the "God of All", everything would turn out all right.

CHAPTER TWO
Leprechauns Among Us

Late that afternoon, PaPa was getting ready for his daily visit with Christy when he suddenly heard a sharp rapping on the kitchen window. PaPa looked up and quickly recognized his good friend, Shamus O'Malley, the leprechaun, and hurried to let him in.

Shamus O'Malley was a very special leprechaun. Like all leprechauns, he was a small fairy. But Shamus had been given great magical powers by the "God of All" to assist him in his many adventures throughout the world helping children in need.

Shamus had been blessed with a disarming smile, a devilish laugh, and one striking feature which was readily apparent to all...his eyes. His eyes were blue with light green edges that always twinkled like Christmas tree lights. Shamus had reddish blonde hair which was just long enough to blow in the breeze. He usually wore a loose fitting green shirt which matched his knee length knickers, gold socks, and black shoes that were topped with large gold square buckles.

Shamus and PaPa
had been friends for a long
time. They first met late one
afternoon when Shamus saw PaPa, the
fireman, on a beach trying to save four baby
Beluga whales which had wandered too close to shore
and were stranded on the beach. The mother whales were
too big to come into the shallow water to save their babies.

PaPa and Shamus, together with many other good people, risked
their lives in the cold, rough waters and led the baby whales safely
into deeper waters back to their mothers. From that day on, Shamus
and these four whales became very special friends.

Shamus was married to Kara Shannon O'Finnegan, a very
pretty leprechaun whom everyone called "Finney". There was not a
leprechaun in the Kingdom, old or young alike, who did not adore her.
She had beautiful, shoulder length red hair mixed with a few strands
of blonde. Her face was soft and her cheeks were sprinkled ever so
gently with freckles. Her skin was fair and her eyes were a rich green
that sparkled like emeralds, conveying the true essence of Finney...
love and gentleness completely wrapped in warmth and sincerity.

Like Shamus, Finney's eyes were full of life and happiness
and a unique warmth of spirit. In Finney, the "God of All"
had given the Kingdom a most beautiful angel who
liked to dress in colorful clothes of green, yellow, pink
and blue, so as to make every day look like spring.

10

"Shamus, what brings you all the way here from Ireland? How are Finney and King O'Flaherty?", PaPa asked.

"Finney is fine, thank you," said Shamus. "But PaPa, the most terrible thing has happened! The Grand Pooka, our most feared enemy, has captured King O'Flaherty and taken his gold and emerald crown. The Grand Pooka sent a messenger to tell us that soon it will come to destroy the Kingdom of the Leprechauns. PaPa, I need your help to get the King back and to save the Kingdom."

"Shamus my good friend, of course I'll help you and the little ones in any way I can," answered PaPa. "But first you must tell me all that has happened."

Shamus sat on the table, crossed his legs, and took a deep breath. "The evil Grand Pooka has come back just the way the legend said it would! While I was away on an adventure helping a child in Mexico, it surprised the King and captured him while he was working in the garden surrounding the Rainbow Tree. If I had been there, this wouldn't have happened!"

"Worst of all PaPa," Shamus continued, "the Grand Pooka's messenger warned me that if I, my very self, do not surrender to him by the next full moon, it will burn down the Rainbow Tree. PaPa, you know what that means to the leprechauns?"

"Yes, Shamus, I do," PaPa gravely answered. "Without the Rainbow Tree, the Kingdom cannot survive and will be lost forever. There will be no more leprechauns with magical powers to help the children of the world."

"I cannot let this happen, PaPa," said Shamus excitedly. "Yet, if I surrender, there will be no leprechaun left who can destroy the Grand Pooka and save the Kingdom."

Shamus paused a moment and then continued, "Before I came to see you we had a meeting of the Kingdom's 'Council of the Wise'." PaPa knew that only the noblest and wisest leprechauns were chosen to sit as members of the Council of the Wise. Shamus continued, "The Council decided that we leprechauns alone cannot destroy the Grand Pooka and save King O'Flaherty. The Council agreed to send me here to ask for your help. PaPa, I'm becoming very angry! I hate the Grand Pooka for what he has done. How could the 'God of All' let this happen?"

"Shamus," PaPa asked, "have you forgotten the basic creed of life? First, to be calm and strong in the face of danger, to do the right thing you cannot act out of hatred, anger or fear. Second, you must never lose faith in yourself. Third, everyone needs help; you must never be afraid to seek the help of your friends. Finally, you must never doubt or lose faith in the 'God of All'."

"PaPa, you have given me new hope!" cried Shamus. "I knew that of all the believers, you would be the one who could help the most. No one has a stronger belief in the goodness of the leprechauns than you. That is why we call you our greatest 'Crediach' (Kra dē ah)...our most honored believer. Together, we must defeat the Grand Pooka and save King O'Flaherty and the Kingdom for all the children in the world who need our help."

"Shamus, we face a most frightful situation, and as always you can count on me," PaPa said. "I will meet you by the Rainbow Tree, on the eve of the next full moon. I know we only have two days left, but I will be there, I promise."

Shamus hugged PaPa and thanked him for his help. Then he hurried back to the Kingdom.

After Shamus left, PaPa couldn't help but worry about the "little ones". Clearly the leprechauns were in great danger. Somehow he would think of a way to help Shamus and the leprechauns. PaPa then got up, put on his jacket and headed for the hospital. Every night since Christy became ill, PaPa had gone to the hospital to tell her a bedtime story, and then sleep in the rocking chair in her room so that she would not be alone.

As PaPa walked on the beach toward St. Francis Hospital, he began thinking again about his dear friend, Shamus O'Malley.

Tonight, he thought, I will tell Christy what I know about the legend called the "Prophecy of Light" and Shamus, the chosen leprechaun. PaPa sadly worried, that soon there might be no more stories to tell about the leprechauns he loved so much.

When PaPa arrived at the hospital, Christy was playing in the sunroom with the other children who were also very sick.

"PaPa!" shouted Christy, "You are finally here. I thought you had forgotten to come and see me."

"Christy, I would never forget!", said PaPa reassuringly. "No matter what happens, I will always do everything possible to see you and be by your bedside to watch over you during the night."

Christy then asked, "PaPa, will you tell me a bedtime story? Please, PaPa?"

"I want to hear a story too," said the little girl, Maria, who was playing dolls with Christy.

"I have an idea," said PaPa to Christy. "How about if I tell all the children a bedtime story called the 'Prophecy of Light'."

Christy replied, "Great!"

"What's a prophecy?" called out one of the children.

PaPa replied, "It means a vision of things to come." Then PaPa said, "Come children, gather around, and I will tell you about the Prophecy, leprechauns, and a special leprechaun named Shamus O'Malley."

With the help of the nurses, the children gathered in the sunroom in a circle in front of PaPa's rocking chair, with Christy sitting snugly on PaPa's lap. The children were from all types of families, Italian, Polish, Jewish, Asian, African-American, Irish, Indian and Hispanic. All of the children were, in many ways, different from each other, but they developed a close bond to one another because each had one thing in common...they were all very sick little children fighting to survive.

"Well now," PaPa began, "Have any of you heard of the little people known as the leprechauns?"

"No!" the children giggled.

"There's no such thing," said Maria.

"That's what I used to think," said PaPa, "but just as I am sitting here, I tell you they surely do exist. They live in a Kingdom all their own in a land called Ireland, inside a beautiful castle with its own river. The Kingdom is located underground beneath the roots of the Rainbow Tree."

CHAPTER THREE
A Doubting Thomas and Pookas

PaPa looked around the room at the wonder in the faces of the children and noticed that one of the boys stood off in the corner by himself. "Say there, young lad! What might your name be?"

"My name is Thomas," answered the little boy.

"Well now, Thomas, why don't you come sit with us and listen to my story about leprechauns?", said PaPa.

"I don't like stories," said Thomas, "and anyway I don't believe in leprechauns!"

"You don't say!" replied PaPa. "Well now, Thomas, a long time ago there was a boy just like you, and he did not believe either. Maybe someday you will change your mind. In the meantime, lad, keep your ears open and you just might hear something you like."

Thomas crossed his arms tightly and turned his back to PaPa. PaPa said to Thomas, "You know lad, I'm often in Ireland."

Thomas responded, "Oh yeah, what part?"

PaPa knew he had caught Thomas off guard, and laughed as he said, "All of me!"

The children all laughed and even Thomas turned and smiled. PaPa smiled back at Thomas and returned to his story.

"The Kingdom is in a town called 'Tralee', located on Tralee Bay, in County Kerry, on the coast of Ireland, facing the great North Atlantic Ocean. The Kingdom is totally underground beneath a tiny strip of land that juts out into the sea like a crooked finger.

Light comes into the Kingdom from the sun and moon, through skylights and polished stones cleverly hidden in the Rainbow Tree. This light makes the Kingdom, its colorful houses, trees, and flowers appear to be like a rainbow of a thousand colors from one end to the other.

Pure water comes into the Kingdom filtered through the roots of the Rainbow Tree. The roots are deep in the earth and pass through the waters of the underground river that flows through the Kingdom.

You see, children, a leprechaun is a small invisible fairy with magical powers. Leprechauns live to be about three hundred years old, and they show themselves only to certain special people called 'Crediachs'. 'Crediach' (Kra dē ah) in the Gaelic language of old Ireland means a believer...one who believes in leprechauns. The crediachs help leprechauns do their good deeds all over the world.

From the beginning of time, the 'God of All' chose leprechauns as 'His' special messengers of faith and good luck. 'He' gave his leprechauns magical powers...powers that come from the light of either the moon or the stars. Only on completely dark nights do leprechauns lose their magical powers.

These little people known as leprechauns dress in green suits or skirts and wear special black or green shoes that let them scamper about in the grass without being heard. Some even wear tiny green hats."

"Oh! I have heard about them before," said one of the children, named Juan. "They are so little that they hide under flowers or mushrooms that grow on the ground."

"That's right," said PaPa, "they are so tiny you need a special eye to see them. But not everyone has that special eye. Only a crediach does. It is considered a precious gift to see the little ones, and it is not a gift to be taken lightly."

PaPa paused a moment, and then in a soft voice said, "Children, the 'God of All' made leprechauns to do only good in the world. They go on many adventures, sent by the 'God of All', to help children in trouble all over the world.

Whenever they hear that a little child is sick, hurt, or needs any kind of help, the leprechauns form a circle, hold their hands together tightly, and pray to the 'God of All' to help the little child. They pray and pray as hard as they can, and when the 'God of All' has heard them, a leprechaun quickly visits the needy child who then feels warm and tingly sensations rushing through his or her body. In just seconds, all of that child's troubles disappear.

20

The only living thing ever feared by a leprechaun is a creature called a 'Pooka'. A Pooka is a heartless monster that has constantly glowing red eyes. It is the glow from their red eyes that lets Pookas see leprechauns. At certain times, when in a rage, Pookas can send out rays of fire from both its eyes and nose.

A Pooka often appears in the shape of a large, hairy animal. It hides its true monstrous form in that of an animal to disguise itself from unsuspecting leprechauns. At other times, Pookas are invisible so that one can only detect their presence by a strange howling noise in a gust of wind.

No one understands why Pookas do not like leprechauns or why they constantly attack them. From the beginning of time, leprechauns have never harmed anyone and have always been friendly to everyone.

The Pookas' home is in a secret hill far to the North of Tralee. No one really knows how many Pookas there are, but King O'Flaherty and all of the leprechauns know that the most fearsome of all of the Pookas is their leader, the Grand Pooka.

The Grand Pooka is an evil ruler who roams the night sky in search of leprechauns to snatch up and take on frightening journeys over the Earth's oceans. The Grand Pooka then carries the leprechauns far away to a secret dark cave. In the cave's darkness, the Grand Pooka places a trance-like spell on the leprechauns which causes them to lose their magical powers.

The Grand
Pooka's spell,
once cast
on a lep-
rechaun,
can only be
broken when the Grand
Pooka is destroyed. This
Grand Pooka has haunted the Kingdom for 293 years, and
far too many leprechauns have been cursed by its spell.

Children, there is only one way to destroy the Grand Pooka.
According to the legend of the 'Prophecy of Light', it requires great
courage on the part of the chosen leprechaun. The Grand Pooka can
be destroyed only when its heart or eyes are pierced by a brilliant
light. But the light, just like the magical powers of leprechauns, can
only come from the moon or a star...and it has to be the most powerful
of all powerful lights."

"Excuse me, PaPa," said Christy's nurse, Ellen-Mary. "This is a wonderful story, but it is very late, and the children need their rest."

"Yes, indeed it is," said PaPa. "Let's all go to bed and I promise to come in a little earlier tomorrow afternoon to tell you more about leprechauns and Shamus O'Malley."

"Please Nurse Ellen-Mary!" the children pleaded, "We want PaPa to finish the story now."

Ellen-Mary, who had the smile of an angel, gently said, "No, not tonight children. PaPa agrees with me that it is late, and as promised, he will come back early tomorrow afternoon to continue the story." Then Ellen-Mary winked at PaPa and helped Christy and the other children to their rooms.

Later that night, Dr. Steve came to Christy's room to talk with PaPa. Dr. Steve was Christy's favorite doctor. He was tall, almost bald, with a big nose and even bigger ears. He was very business-like, but he was a kind and gentle man who adored Christy. From the first time Dr. Steve saw Christy, he promised to use all of his skill to care for and treat her. Privately, he feared that it would not be enough.

"Well, Dr. Steve," asked PaPa, "has the new medicine made a difference yet? Is Christy getting better?"

"It does not look like the medicine is working, but it is still too early to tell for sure," said Dr. Steve. "The next few days will be very important. We've done all we can to help her, now we must wait and see."

"Then, I must go to the hospital's chapel and say a prayer to the 'God of All'," said PaPa.

"I don't believe that will help. If Christy gets better, it will be due to the new medicine," said Dr. Steve.

"Well now," said PaPa, "I'm afraid I have to disagree with you, Dr. Steve. Prayer is far more powerful than you know."

"Pray if you wish, PaPa," said Dr. Steve and then he closed the door behind him.

23

Early that evening, Nurse Ellen-Mary came into Christy's room to check on her. She told PaPa, who was sitting next to Christy's bed, that "the children are excited about your story, even Thomas."

"Ellen-Mary," PaPa asked, "What can you tell me about little Thomas? I don't recall that I have ever seen anyone here to visit him."

"He has no family," answered Ellen-Mary sadly, "Thomas was orphaned as a baby. He has the same sickness that Christy has, but the new medicine appears to be helping him more than Christy. Hopefully, he will soon be able to return to the orphanage."

"He's a feisty young lad now, isn't he?" asked PaPa.

"Thomas has had a very tough life and has a hard time getting close to people," answered Ellen-Mary. "He gets into mischief quite a bit, but he really is a good child and very kindhearted. Be patient with him. You'll come to love him very much, just as I do."

On her way out the door Ellen-Mary stopped, turned to PaPa, and said, "Tonight I too will say a special prayer for Christy to get well."

PaPa thanked her.

Later that night as Christy lay sleeping in her bed, PaPa took a picture of Sandy, Christy's grandma and his dear departed wife, from his wallet and quietly spoke to her.

"And what would you have me do now, Sandy? I know that I should not be leaving Christy alone at a time like this, but on the other hand, I can not fail to help the leprechauns in their desperate time of need. It's a bit of a problem that I find myself in right now."

PaPa was very tired and while still holding the picture in his hands, his weary eyes closed.

CHAPTER FOUR
The Legend

While PaPa slept in the hospital chair, he had the most incredible dream. He dreamt that Sandy told him to go to the attic at home and find the Shamus and Finney leprechaun dolls that their daughter, Betty, had played with as a child. In his dream, Sandy told him that these dolls, while gently tucked into Christy's arms as she slept, would keep her safe and watch over her while he was far away in the Kingdom of the Leprechauns.

The next morning when PaPa went home, he climbed the worn but sturdy stairway to the attic. Boxes and bags lay scattered about the room.

"It will take forever to find anything up here!" PaPa said to himself. And then he spotted an old wooden toy box in the corner. After clearing away the clutter, he opened the lid of the toy box. Sitting on top of the pile of old toys were the two tiny leprechaun dolls, Shamus and Finney.

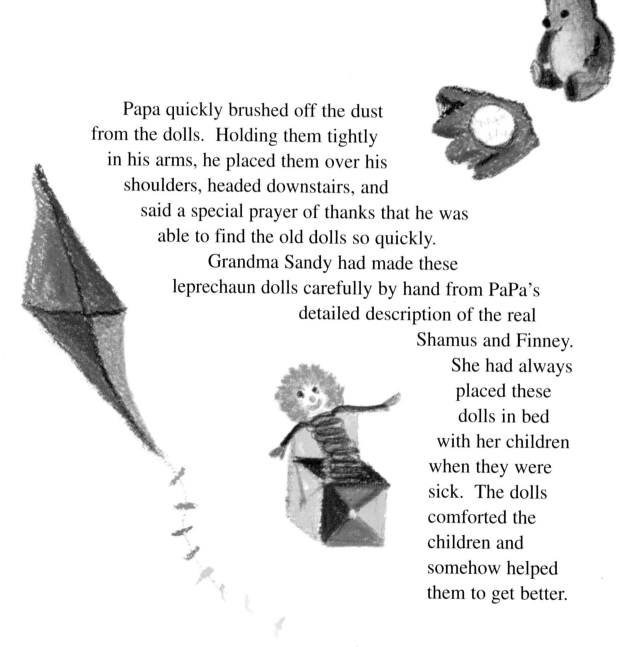

Papa quickly brushed off the dust
from the dolls. Holding them tightly
in his arms, he placed them over his
shoulders, headed downstairs, and
said a special prayer of thanks that he was
able to find the old dolls so quickly.
Grandma Sandy had made these
leprechaun dolls carefully by hand from PaPa's
detailed description of the real
Shamus and Finney.
She had always
placed these
dolls in bed
with her children
when they were
sick. The dolls
comforted the
children and
somehow helped
them to get better.

28

Later that afternoon, as promised, PaPa gathered the children around him in the hospital's sunroom to continue telling his story. He saw that the children were staring at him with trancelike gazes. At the same time, he noticed that Thomas had quietly crawled very close to his rocking chair. PaPa warmly grinned and winked at Thomas, and then began...

"As you now know, the leprechauns live in an undergound Kingdom beneath the Rainbow Tree which provides the Kingdom with all its light and water. Everyone knows that without the Rainbow Tree, the Kingdom could not survive."

PaPa paused a few seconds and then said, "Now children, before I continue the story about Shamus O'Malley, I must tell you what happened a long long time ago beyond the misty space of one hundred and fifty years when the Grand Pooka and his army of little Pookas attacked the Kingdom of Leprechauns. Shamus was only three years old at the time. His father, Sean O'Malley, was chosen by the Council of Wise to lead the leprechauns into battle and defeat the Grand Pooka. Shamus' mother, Margaret, was with Sean during the battle. To this very day, no one knows how Sean and Margaret fought off the Grand Pooka and saved the Kingdom. Everyone believes some sort of miracle took place.

30

The leprechauns who survived that great battle all thought the Grand Pooka was dead...but it was not. The Grand Pooka had been badly wounded, but it dragged itself off into the night having captured Sean and Margaret. The Grand Pooka growled and vowed that it would return. Next time, the Kingdom of the Leprechauns would be destroyed forever.

King O'Flaherty had just recently told Shamus that both his Mother and Father were captured by the Grand Pooka and were never seen again.

The legend of the 'Prophecy of Light' foretold that the Grand Pooka would attack the Kingdom twice within one hundred and fifty years, and that only a chosen leprechaun might be able to save the Kingdom in the last great battle.

The legend was first mysteriously revealed over a thousand years ago to the Kingdom's third king, Darcey O'Toole. The legend said that when the forces of darkness and evil came to destroy the Kingdom of the Leprechauns, there would be one leprechaun among all the others, whose faith and courage might be great enough to save the Kingdom.

King O'Flaherty was the only
one in the Kingdom who knew, deep in his heart, that when the Grand
Pooka came again to attack the Kingdom, Shamus O'Malley, the only
living son of the chosen leprechaun Sean, would be the one the legend
said might be able to save the Kingdom. The King also knew that the
'God of All' had filled Shamus with special faith and courage to face
this awesome challenge.

King O'Flaherty told just one other person about the secrets of the
legend of the 'Prophecy of Light'. He told me. For the King knew
that when the time came, Shamus might need my help. The legend
did not say, nor does anyone know, whether or not the
Kingdom will be saved!"

PaPa paused and took a deep breath, then he told the
wide-eyed children in a grave tone, "Sadly, I have just
learned that only a few days ago King O'Flaherty was
captured by the Grand Pooka. The time for Shamus to
defend the Kingdom is now at hand!"

Bedtime had long passed and all the children went quickly to
their own beds. PaPa tucked Christy in himself. She was so tired, she
fell asleep immediately. PaPa gently placed the Shamus and Finney
dolls in Christy's arms and prayed to the "God of All" that they would
protect her in his absence.

The eve of the next full moon had arrived much too quickly for PaPa. He kissed Christy and quickly left her room to catch his airplane to Ireland, which left in only one hour.

Later that evening Dr. Steve visited Christy's room.

"That's strange," said Dr. Steve to himself, "PaPa is always here beside Christy during the night. Well anyway, Christy is sleeping and appears to be doing well." Dr. Steve gently pulled back the sheets to check the strength of Christy's heartbeat. In doing so, he accidently moved the Shamus and Finney dolls underneath the sheets to the foot of her bed.

Very early the next morning, while Christy slept, the hospital's housekeeping staff, moving Christy ever so gently, quietly changed her sheets and blankets. No one noticed that the Shamus and Finney dolls were wrapped up in the sheets and were on their way to the hospital laundry.

CHAPTER FIVE

The Gathering Storm

*F*ar to the North, storm clouds were gathering over the land of the Pookas. Darkness was everywhere. The Grand Pooka roared with delight as all its plans and preparations were finally ready. The time was at hand for its long awaited triumph over the leprechauns. Soon the Grand Pooka would fulfill the darkest secrets of the legend of the "Prophecy of Light". It would get revenge for the defeat of the Pookas at the hands of Shamus' father one hundred and fifty years ago.

An evil smile crossed the face of the Grand Pooka as it thought to itself confidently, "Shamus and all the leprechauns know that I have captured their beloved King O'Flaherty. They also know that I now have the powers of his gold and emerald crown. Surely the leprechauns must be terrified. The eve of the next full moon is upon us...soon I will begin my attack."

The Grand Pooka had waited one hundred and fifty years for this night to happen. It had sought out the advice of all the evil and dark

forces it had ever
known to assure
success
against
Shamus and
the leprechauns.
It did not matter that
Shamus had not surrendered, for the Grand Pooka's
battle plan was complete.

The Grand Pooka believed its plan to be foolproof. With one
night of terror, it would destroy the Rainbow Tree and the Kingdom of
Leprechauns. Only the chosen leprechaun, Shamus O'Malley, stood
between it and victory. It would have the special powers of the King's
gold and emerald crown when it attacked Shamus and the Rainbow
Tree. It would cast a spell and turn all the leprechauns into many evil
and bad little Pookas, just like the Grand Pooka. They would join the
Grand Pooka in making the world an unhappy place for everyone to
live in.

The leprechauns would never again be filled with joy, merry-making and kindness. They would soon all be little monstrous Pookas. Soon they would be messengers of evil for the Grand Pooka, not messengers of goodness for the "God of All". Now, all the Grand Pooka had to decide was what evil shape to take in the battle to come. Its victory would be swift and easy.

PaPa, before he knew it, found himself staring at the Rainbow Tree. The color of its leaves and branches were as magnificent as ever and were arranged in such a way as to make the tree appear as a giant rainbow. It was a sight PaPa had always cherished and one he would never forget.

As PaPa approached the entrance to the Kingdom, hidden underneath the Rainbow Tree, he was met by Shamus. The Council of the Wise had just met again and all agreed that Shamus was indeed the chosen leprechaun, foretold by the "Prophecy of Light." Shamus must fight the Grand Pooka and try to save the Kingdom. Finney and the other leprechauns would await the outcome of the battle in the underground Kingdom.

CHAPTER SIX
A World Before Unknown

PaPa and Shamus stood underneath the Rainbow Tree keeping a watchful eye for the coming of the Grand Pooka. Heavy clouds with thunder and lightning made it the darkest night either of them could remember.

Then, suddenly, from out of the dark clouds came a giant fireball circling in the night sky, building speed to attack and burn down the Rainbow Tree. The Grand Pooka held King O'Flaherty's gold and emerald crown in the middle of the fireball. Shamus and PaPa had guessed right! The Grand Pooka had taken the shape of a fireball, which appeared to be bigger than the sun itself.

PaPa and Shamus had made plans to protect the Rainbow Tree from being burned down. PaPa, the fireman, devised the plan, but Shamus, with his magical powers to speak with the animals, was the key to saving the Rainbow Tree.

There was little time to act.
Shamus called to his special friends,
Daniel, Heather, Ryan, and Bridget. Each of
the beautiful Beluga whales, now
fully grown, swam furiously to four separate
underwater sea caves, two on each side of the strip of land which
contained the leprechaun Kingdom. The underground river that ran
through the Kingdom emptied into the sea from these caves. Water
from the sea and underground river flowed through
the roots of the Rainbow Tree.

Daniel, Heather, Ryan,
and Bridget were now each about
16 feet long and weighed close to 3000
pounds. The large whales blew as much sea
water as they possibly could, back into
the underground river, pushing
the sea water back through the roots
of and into the hundred branches
of the Rainbow Tree until the
branches were ready to burst.

The fireball Grand Pooka
started its attack on the Rainbow
Tree. It charged furiously, and as it got
closer, the fire and heat from the fireball began to burn the leaves of
the Rainbow Tree and all the flowers around it.

PaPa and Shamus were near collapse from the intense heat and
flames of the fireball. But PaPa knew that he had to wait for just the
right time.

PaPa and Shamus bravely stood their ground as the charging Grand Pooka fireball was about to strike the Rainbow Tree. Just when the heat and flames from the fireball became too much to bear, PaPa hollered out in a loud voice, "Now!". It was a signal to Shamus, who then loudly shouted to the Beluga whales to blow sea water one more time, as hard as they could, into the underground river. Suddenly, each branch of the Rainbow Tree exploded all at once with sea water, like powerful firehoses, completely spraying the Grand Pooka fireball and instantly causing it to evaporate into a steam cloud. Thanks to PaPa and Shamus, the Rainbow Tree had been saved! PaPa collapsed to the ground and did not move.

The Grand Pooka was totally surprised when it was struck by the sea water from the Rainbow Tree. In its shock, it dropped King O'Flaherty's gold and emerald crown, which fell safely to the ground next to Shamus. Shamus felt thrilled and relieved. Then in an instant, he fell exhausted and unconscious to the ground.

In a short time,
darkness had
fallen
over the
Kingdom.
Shamus, still dazed,
slowly rolled over and got
to his feet. He saw PaPa lying motionless on the ground.
Shamus was saddened as he thought his good friend was dead.
Then, the greatest fear Shamus had ever known overpowered him.
Instantly his heart stopped beating and he could not breathe. He
thought the Grand Pooka had been destroyed! It was not! For in the
dark night sky he saw that the Grand Pooka had reformed itself from a
steam cloud into the most horrible of all beasts.

Shamus, filled with fear and despair, was now alone and helpless.
Worst of all, the steam from the fireball and the thick dark clouds,
called together this night by the Grand Pooka, shut out all the light
from the moon and stars. Shamus would no longer have any magical
powers. The end of the Kingdom was near. He had failed King
O'Flaherty, Finney, and all the other leprechauns. Shamus picked up
King O'Flaherty's gold and emerald crown. Then he ran and fell on
the ground next to where PaPa lay.

44

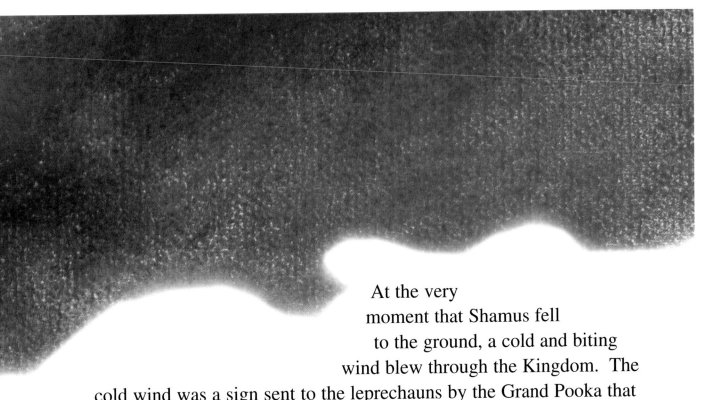

At the very
moment that Shamus fell
to the ground, a cold and biting
wind blew through the Kingdom. The
cold wind was a sign sent to the leprechauns by the Grand Pooka that
its final attack was near and that the Kingdom would soon be
destroyed. The Grand Pooka was winning the battle above.

The leprechauns now lost hope that the Kingdom would survive
and fear filled their hearts. The frightened leprechauns ran in panic in
all directions. Chaos was everywhere! Where would they go or hide
when the Grand Pooka entered the Kingdom? What would the Grand
Pooka do to them?

Why had the "God of All" abandoned them?!

An evil smile again crossed the face of the Grand Pooka as it
thought of how it would capture Shamus and take him on a frightful
ride in the night's sky to the secret dark cave where Shamus would
lose his magical powers forever. The "Prophecy of Light" was a
legend that would have a dark ending. The nonsense about a chosen
leprechaun saving the Kingdom must have been dreamed up by
ancient leprechaun kings to give false hope to the leprechauns. The
leprechauns could no longer save their Kingdom, especially now that
the Grand Pooka knew Shamus and the leprechauns had lost faith in
the "God of All".

CHAPTER SEVEN
Tingling Sensations

Shamus' eyes slowly opened. The horror he would soon face did not bother him, but failing his beloved King and all of the leprechauns filled him with sadness and anger. Shamus hated the Grand Pooka as he thought of what had happened to his parents. He could not understand why the "God of All" had abandoned him in his gravest hour of need.

Suddenly, Shamus heard a song, and a beautiful young woman appeared in a cloud of mist. The beautiful young woman softly called Shamus by his name.

Shamus immediately thought it was Finney, but it was not her voice. Was his mind playing tricks on him?

All of a sudden, Shamus' entire body shivered and he stood tall. Shamus then recognized that the beautiful young woman's face and soft voice were actually that of his mother, Margaret, now a very beautiful angel.

Margaret quickly calmed her son, Shamus, and told him that in order to defeat the Grand Pooka he must first rid himself of the evil thoughts of anger and hatred. These thoughts are wrong and were planted in his mind by the forces of evil to confuse him. Only by ridding himself of these thoughts could he hope to overcome evil.

Shamus' mother then told him that he must have faith in himself, faith in all the Kingdom's leprechauns for he needed their help too, and finally faith in the "God of All". His mother rekindled Shamus' courage.

Finally, the angel, Margaret, told Shamus that he must quickly go to the highest point of land above the Kingdom and lift King O'Flaherty's gold and emerald crown as high as was possible in both of his hands.

Then Margaret left as quickly as she had appeared.

Suddenly Shamus felt marvelous and warm tingling sensations throughout his entire body. He felt stronger and braver than he ever had before.

It was now time to act!!

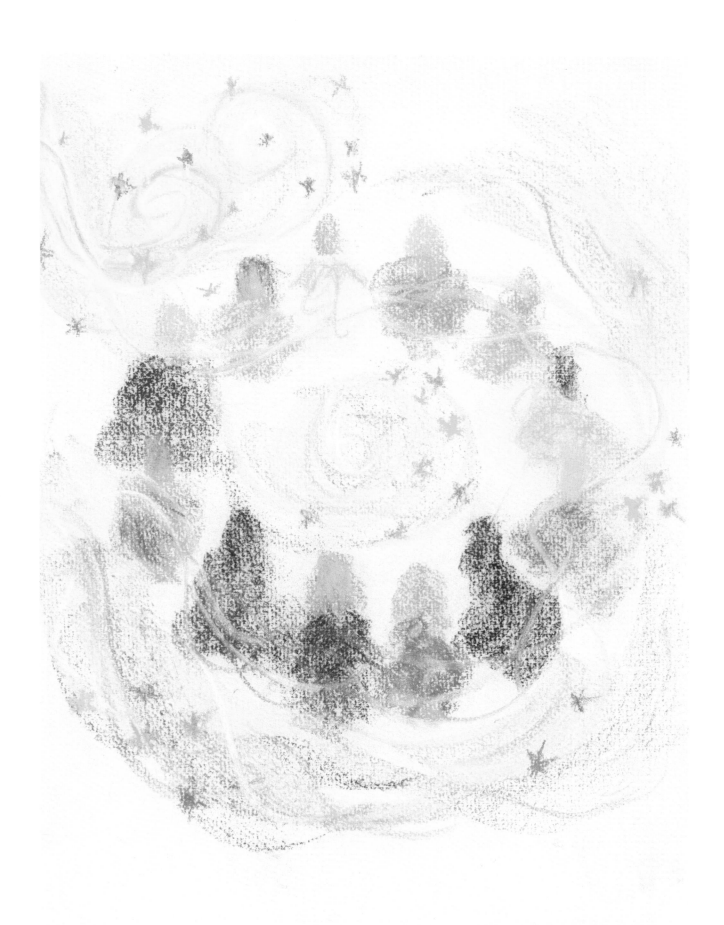

CHAPTER EIGHT
The Circle of Hands

In all its fury the Grand Pooka started its charge toward Shamus. Dark moving clouds were driven across the night's sky by powerful winds. Rain and lightning flashed everywhere providing cover for the advancing Grand Pooka.

With every passing second, the attacking Grand Pooka moved closer. At times, it advanced as a howling wind and at other times in the form of a monster goat with glowing red eyes. Its total evilness terrified Shamus. The Grand Pooka roared in all its ugliness, spitting out flames of fire from its nose and eyes, directly at Shamus.

Meanwhile, undergound in the Kingdom, Finney, driven by her love for Shamus and her own fears, walked alone in the darkness. As she walked, she began to silently pray to the "God of All". Finney looked up towards the heavens and closed her eyes. Suddenly, a vision appeared in her mind and she could see everything that was happening to Shamus above the Kingdom. Her quivering body, now filled with fear, told her the vision was real and tears fell down her soft cheeks. As the vision began to fade, Finney could see a large gathering of the Kingdom's leprechauns. What could this mean?

Mysteriously, Finney suddenly felt warm tingling sensations throughout her entire body. Immediately the tingling sensations restored a quiet calmness, filling Finney with faith, trust, and hope.

She then ran as fast as she could to find the other members of the Council of the Wise. Finney instructed the Council members to gather all the leprechauns together in the Kingdom's central park.

In the park, Finney told the leprechauns about her vision in which she learned that PaPa had collapsed and that Shamus stood alone and helpless against the fury of the Grand Pooka. Finney then told them that she now believed all the leprechauns could help save the Kingdom. Each leprechaun would have to have absolute trust and faith in each other.

Upon the command of Finney, all of the leprechauns in the Kingdom formed a giant circle by holding each other's outstretched hands. Each leprechaun then silently looked up at Finney.

Finney, in a soft but confident voice, said to all the leprechauns, "Our only chance to save the Kingdom is to once again believe in each other and our magical powers, and to remember the great faith we have in the 'God of All'. The 'God of All' will not abandon us."

Finney continued to reassure them saying, "King O'Flaherty and Shamus always believed that when each leprechaun in the Kingdom stood together, they could overcome any evil."

Finney knew that if all the leprechauns truly believed this, their faith and trust would send forth strong ripples of hope and renewed strength to Shamus...and would also serve as prayers for help to the 'God of All'.

The doubters became believers, and each believer soon believed more than he or she had ever believed before.

Soon a golden glow in the form of a halo started to rise, first from the body and then from the head of each leprechaun. Each of the halos then joined together to become one enormous halo of unusually warm and intense golden light, which then glowed over all of the leprechauns in the circle of hands.

Finney, inspired by the tingling sensations, had accomplished the impossible. The leprechauns' faith and trust in each other had been restored, hope abounded everywhere. The darkness in the Kingdom was replaced with the golden light.

Finney hoped it was not too late.

CHAPTER NINE
Let There Be Light

Shamus did exactly as his mother, the angel Margaret, had told him. He ran to the highest point above the Kingdom and climbed the large pile of rocks on the cliff located nearby on the seacoast. Giant waves pounded the shore. The spray of the white-water splashed high onto Shamus, but he stood firm in the fury of the winds and rains with King O'Flaherty's gold and emerald crown held high in both of his hands.

The wicked Grand Pooka charged as fast as it could toward Shamus. It thought to itself how ridiculous Shamus looked standing high on the rocks holding something high above his head in his outstretched hands.

The Grand
Pooka did not know that
Shamus was holding the gold and
emerald crown, which
contained three special emeralds.
Only the "God of All" knew the full
power of these precious
emeralds. For it was "He"
who long ago made a special gift
of the gold and emerald crown to
the first leprechaun king.

The emeralds always glowed in
the dark with a soft green light. They
did this whether they were in the possession
of good or evil doers. The Grand Pooka
had mistakenly believed the glowing emerald
crown would add special
powers to its own evilness. It was
wrong. For the "God of All"
made these emeralds so that
they would only have special
powers for those who did good in
the world.

Underground in the Kingdom, the halo of golden light that glowed over all the leprechauns in the circle of hands formed itself into a rushing flash of golden light. The speed of the flash of golden light was slightly faster than that of the charging Grand Pooka and its forces of evil.

The flash of golden light quickly rose through the skylights and polished stones hidden in the branches of the Rainbow Tree and headed directly for Shamus and the gold and emerald crown he held high in his hands.

Shamus watched the golden light reflect off the gold and emerald crown held high in his hands. In amazement, he saw the golden light become charged like a bolt of lightning, becoming so bright that he had to turn his face away until the light disappeared into the night's angry and dark clouds.

Finney ran as fast as she could after the flash of golden light up the stairs of the Kingdom, but she could not keep pace with the fast-moving light.

Just as the golden light disappeared into the night's clouds, Finney reached the land above the Kingdom. It was the darkest night she had ever seen. For a moment she fell exhausted to her knees and looked up. Every inch of her body trembled as she watched the horrible beast, Grand Pooka with all its evil forces, advance to destroy Shamus.

As Finney turned her head, she saw PaPa still lying nearby on the ground. Finney gently shook PaPa and immediately his eyes opened.

He was still alive! PaPa quickly reached out and held Finney's hands, softly whispering to her, "We must have faith."

Then, all of a sudden, it happened! With the Grand Pooka only twenty feet away from Shamus and its final victory, the night sky's dark clouds were forced apart. The charged flash of golden light had reached the moon hidden behind the dark clouds. Reflecting off the moon's surface it was changed into the most powerful moonbeam ever created, which easily separated the dark clouds and headed, with tremendous speed, directly back to where Shamus stood.

All the forces of evil, the dark clouds, the furious winds and rain could not withstand the incredible power of this, the most powerful of all moonbeams. Just as the fire-breathing monster goat Grand Pooka reached out to capture and destroy Shamus, the powerful moonbeam reflected off the emeralds in the gold crown directly into the Grand Pooka's eyes. Flashes of light and sparks flew everywhere.

The moonbeam had such power and force that it caused the entire body of the Grand Pooka to explode into billions of ashes, scattered for all time by the winds into the deep waters of the North Sea. It was, at last, over!!

All the other little Pookas quickly surrendered to Shamus and returned King O'Flaherty to the Kingdom unharmed and in good spirits. The little Pookas would, forever more, do only good deeds with their new leprechaun friends.

0   1

CHAPTER TEN
Faith Restored

All the leprechauns celebrated in the Kingdom like never before. PaPa did not stay for the celebration. He returned right away to the hospital to see Christy. When PaPa arrived, Dr. Steve was in Christy's room.

"PaPa, we have been looking everywhere for you," said Dr. Steve. "We have some terrible news. Christy's sickness has gotten much worse. She is burning with fever and is in a coma, unable to talk or eat. I am afraid she will not make it through the night."

"Please do not talk like that, Dr. Steve," pleaded PaPa. "We must never give up hope. I must pray to the 'God of All'."

Just as PaPa started to leave Christy's room, he noticed that the Shamus and Finney dolls were gone. He shouted, "Where are the dolls I left here to protect Christy?"

"PaPa," replied Dr. Steve with a puzzled look on his face, "I don't know. The nurses looked for them everywhere but couldn't find them."

PaPa cried out, "Christy is defenseless! Someone must find those dolls right away! Christy needs help from the 'God of All' and his special messengers."

PaPa wondered where Nurse Ellen-Mary was. If she had been here, he was certain this would not have happened.

PaPa knew that there was only one thing left to do. He went downstairs to the hospital's chapel. It was a simple chapel with only a few benches, softly lit by many candles.

In the darkened silence, PaPa knelt and began to pray. After some time passed, he was touched on the shoulder by Dr. Steve. Dr. Steve told PaPa, "I have come to say that I am sorry for not being able to save Christy."

PaPa replied, "Dr Steve, the new medicine has failed. I am praying to the only one who I believe can now save Christy...the 'God of All'."

Dr. Steve said, "I told you before. I don't believe in the 'God of All'."

PaPa couldn't believe what he had just heard and looked at Dr. Steve and asked, "How can you say such a thing? You are a fine young man and a gifted doctor whom the 'God of All' has blessed many times."

64

Dr. Steve answered, "I stopped believing in the 'God of All' when my wife Judy and I could not have our own children. We begged 'Him' for many years to help us have children. But the 'God of All' didn't care about us!"

On the bench in front of PaPa were large drops of tears; tears that had flowed for Christy and now also for Dr. Steve.

PaPa turned to Dr. Steve and said, "My dear friend, why do you love Christy and all of these sick children so much? Don't you love these children as if they were your own?

Dr. Steve, you love Christy and the sick children so much because the 'God of All' intended that for now, they be your only children. You must understand that you have been blessed in so many ways because you have used your special gifts as the 'God of All' intended, to care for his sick children. I am quite sure that the 'God of All' only chooses the most gifted among us to care for the sick children that 'He' loves so much."

Dr. Steve found himself kneeling next to PaPa, with one of PaPa's strong arms around his shoulders. Dr. Steve understood what PaPa said and then he realized that he had always believed in the "God of All"...but like so many others, he had just lost faith in "Him" for all of the wrong reasons.

PaPa's words touched Dr. Steve's heart. Dr. Steve could not hold back his tears any longer, tears which fell down his cheeks like heavy rain down a windowpane, splashing next to those of PaPa's already on the bench below.

PaPa's and Dr. Steve's tears mixed together on the bench and faith and trust in the "God of All" filled Dr. Steve's heart and spirit. PaPa and Dr. Steve, silently prayed together... for Christy. Would their faith be enough to save Christy? Dr. Steve quietly left the chapel and headed back to Christy's room.

While PaPa continued to pray in the chapel, Ellen-Mary found the Shamus and Finney dolls sitting on top of the clothes dryer in the hospital laundry room and quickly placed them back with Christy. Each was squeaky clean.

PaPa did not notice that Shamus was sitting on the wooden bench behind him as he prayed, and that someone else had crept out of his bed and was hiding in the chapel. That someone was Thomas, who until this moment, did not believe in leprechauns.

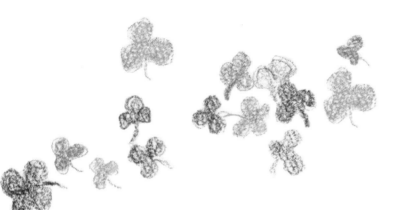

Shamus tapped a surprised PaPa on the shoulder and said, "PaPa what has happened? All was well when you left us a short while ago. I felt a strange sadness in my heart during the celebration and I knew that the 'God of All' wanted me to come and see you."

"My little friend, I am losing my beloved Christy as we speak," said PaPa sadly. "There is nothing more I can do. I am very sad and upset. I can't understand why the 'God of All' is doing this to me."

PaPa, now you have forgotten life's basic creed," replied Shamus. "You know that anger will not help. Keep faith in yourself. Your friends and I are here to help you. Above all, never lose faith in the 'God of All'!"

Huddled in the corner, Thomas could hear PaPa talking with someone but he could not see who it was. He crept around the bench to get a better look. When Thomas saw the little leprechaun, Shamus, he could hardly believe his eyes. He sat very quietly while PaPa and Shamus talked and then prayed together.

Thomas saw the sadness in PaPa's eyes and wished that there was something he could do to help. Then in the wink of an eye, Shamus grabbed the surprised Thomas by the hand and said, "Come on young lad, you and I have work to do."

Suddenly PaPa began to feel warm tingling sensations throughout his body. PaPa immediately left the chapel and ran to Christy's room, completely unprepared for what he would find. Around Christy's bed were all the children from the hospital standing together, forming a circle with their little hands joined. With them were Shamus, Finney, Ellen-Mary, and Dr. Steve. Tears formed in PaPa's eyes as Thomas smiled and held out his hand for PaPa to join them.

All together they closed their eyes tightly and prayed as hard as they could for little Christy to get better. Peeking through one eye, Thomas searched the room for signs that the circle of hands was working. Soon everyone in the circle of hands began to feel warm tingling sensations running through their bodies, and when they looked out the window they saw a bright moonbeam, sparkling with thousands of brilliant lights.

Even Dr. Steve was amazed by what was happening. Suddenly, Christy sat up in her bed, rubbed the sleep from her eyes, and said, "Hi, PaPa. Have you come to finish telling us the story about Shamus and the 'Prophecy of Light'? Please hold me and I know everything will be all right." Everyone cheered and cried tears of joy as PaPa hugged Christy.

CHAPTER ELEVEN
Once Upon a Teardrop

Later in the week, PaPa was told by Dr. Steve that Christy's sickness had completely disappeared and that she would soon be able to go home. It was truly a miracle. PaPa was filled with joy as he held Christy on his lap.

Christy turned to PaPa and said, "You see PaPa, the 'God of All' and Dr. Steve have made me better just like you said they would. Thank you, Dr. Steve."

"Yes, and we have many others to thank for your good fortune as well, including this young lad right here," PaPa said pointing to Thomas, who was peeking around the doorway.

"Come right in, Thomas," said PaPa. "We would like to thank you for helping Shamus, Finney, and all of the children form the circle of hands that helped make Christy better. Remember that people who give to others always receive far more in return. Wonderful things will happen for you too, Thomas!"

"They already have," said Thomas, "I will be going to a new home tomorrow."

"Thomas, my lad, this is wonderful news," cried PaPa. "I am so happy for you."

"That's right," said Dr. Steve, "Thomas will not be going back to the orphanage. He will be coming home with me. Judy and I want Thomas to be our son."

Only King O'Flaherty knew that someday an orphan named Thomas would become one of the world's most famous of all crediachs.

As Dr. Steve and Thomas were leaving the room, Ellen-Mary entered and warmly hugged and kissed Christy. Before she left the room, she turned to PaPa and said goodbye. PaPa blew her a kiss and winked at her.

Winks were secret signs between the "God of All",
angels, leprechauns, and crediachs. It meant that all was or
soon would be well.

The hospital had never seen a celebration like the one that they
had that afternoon. There were balloons and special treats for all of
the children, and laughter echoed through the halls. Quietly and
unknown to all, during the celebration, Shamus and Finney placed
shamrocks underneath the pillows of all the children in St. Francis
Hospital. The shamrocks would be their sign of hope and good luck.

Later that afternoon, PaPa said goodbye to Shamus and Finney, who quickly returned to the Kingdom. Once there, Shamus and Finney took a few moments that night to be alone together on the beach.

The "God of All" playfully pushed two stars, causing them to tumble from the night sky and become two spectacular shooting stars. The two shooting stars then crisscrossed and collided just above the night's beautiful moonbeam, bursting and showering on Shamus and Finney warm sparkling lights.

Far away on a beach in Connecticut, PaPa and Christy saw the same two shooting stars collide and were also showered with their warm sparkling lights.

The "God of All" smiled down on everyone as all was, at last, well. "He" was always happy to send tingling sensations or inspiration to those in need of them. A tear of happiness fell from "His" eye because "His" special messengers, the leprechauns, and Christy were at last safe and well.

And for Shamus and Finney, the adventure was just beginning.